Jingle
A Christmas Anthology

by

The Medicine Hat Rhyme & Reason Writers' Club

Copyright

Table of Contents

Preface

The Medicine Hat Rhyme and Reason Writers' Club is thrilled to present our first annual holiday anthology "Jingles". This book is a product of many hours spent planning, writing and bringing words to life so that we can share them with you. Everything a writer creates feels like it's a piece of them, and this project is no different. It's a labour of love that we offer to you, our fellow readers and lovers of words.

There are so many other writers out there who have their own stories or verse inside of them. If you are one of those writers, we invite you to join us to fulfill your own writing goals! Reach out to us on our Facebook page or visit our website medicinehatwriters.org to find meeting dates and club information.

As a small organization full of dreamers, so much of what we do is only possible with your support, and we thank you from the bottom of our hearts. We hope you enjoy this book for years to come, and wish you many warm, joyous memories!

Happy holidays!

The Art of Gift Giving

by

Kerry Bennett

Gift giving is an art.

I'm not talking about grabbing something off a shelf and tossing it in a gift bag with a little tissue and a hastily signed tag. But real, thoughtful gift giving—on the same scale as a fine painting, artisan baking or antique car restoration. The kind of gift that elicits a spontaneous intake of breath, an unrepressed smile and brightened eyes that say, "It's perfect!"

Unfortunately like scherenschnitte and hand written letters, the art of gift giving appears destined for extinction. (What's scherenschnitte you ask? My point exactly.)

Now, you may argue, we give gifts all the time. And that's true. Gifts for birthdays and weddings and graduations. Gifts for yearly holidays. Gifts for a new job, a new house, a new baby. And guilt gifts— possibly the most expensive of all.

But does a tally of receipts or the balance on our credit card equal exceptional gift giving?

Hardly!

Today gift giving, like fast food dinners and speed dating, is all about expediency. Jam-packed lives and overstuffed schedules may be blamed for this clamoring for convenience.

But it comes with a cost, not only to our wallet but also our relationships.

This social offering designed to communicate our deepest feelings for one another has been reduced to the equivalent of paint-by-number sets, boxed cake mixes and snap together car models.

Unfortunately, there is nothing like Christmas to remind us of how good or bad we are at gift giving.

The dread of busy malls or late night online shopping sprees can douse our holiday spirit before we've even begun.

Have we taken this simple social interaction and turned it into a chore? Are we missing the point of gift giving? Should we ban the practice all together?

Not yet, say psychologists who find gift giving has a complex and important role in our human interactions. It helps define relationships—who is important in our lives and who is not. It helps strengthen bonds with family members and between friends. And in some cases, the kind of gifts we give can signal the end of a relationship.

Even more important, researchers say it may be the gift giver that benefits most from the act. Giving gifts helps strengthen feelings of caring toward others.*

So what will it take to resuscitate the art and reap the benefits?

First, we have to recognize great gifts do not always require great sums of money. Sometimes it is the simplest and smallest thing that means the most.

Second is time. And that's where the biggest problem lies. It takes time to listen and to watch. Time to ask about another's interests and ambitions. Time to find that gift that truly expresses your feelings.

Yes, some of us are better at it than others. Sometimes we get it right. And sometimes we don't. But like all fine arts, gift giving is not one to give up on. Because every once in a while you'll know you mastered it.

*A Gift That Gives Right Back? The Giving Itself by Tara Parker-Pop, Dec. 11, 2007, New York Times.

The Tower of the Flock

by

Jim Burk

I had reached the halfway point on Migdol Eder's slope when I met Caleb coming down; my first experience with a shepherd leaving his watch before transferring the ram horn from his hand to mine.

"Have a good sleep," he sneered, slapping the horn into my waiting palm and continued striding downward. No mention of conditions so far, just the jibe. I'd never slept on watch and he knew it.

Should report him, I thought. *Would do it too, if I weren't second youngest. Worst time ever for a gap in the watch, what with riff-raff of all stripes mixing with Jews coming from places as far away as Alexandria and Babylon to honour the Festival of Booths.*

Festival of booths! I stumbled, mind filling with regrets. Regrets! Regrets that I'd never gone to the temple as an adult. Never worshipped Jehovah in the inner court, and, while I remained a shepherd, never would. Being a shepherd meant being unclean, and hence unfit for entry into the temple.

Regaining my focus on reaching the crest, I circled, eyes searching the pastures and surroundings for possible dangers; pastures where the boy, David, who would be king, once calmed his own flocks with harp and song.

Dodging through the scattered hewn stone remaining from an ancient crumbled tower, still known as Migdol Eder, or Tower of the Flock, I mounted a rough, stone platform for a more panoramic view of the valley below.

The moon shone, nearly full, spilling shadow across

nearby Bethlehem and silhouetting the more distant walls of Jerusalem. As a boy I'd lived in that town. Attended Beth Sefer in the local synagogue, and roamed its streets until my father's death and sale of our home. Would new owners have purchased palm branches as my father had done? Would they have taken those palm branches to the roof of our house and woven them into temporary shelters as homage to the sacred festival?

A remembered sense of childish joy swept over me. A memory of sharing such a shelter with family and glimpsing stars through openings in the woven branches. Most of all though, I remembered father's stories and quotations from the words of Moses. Through those stories I'd developed a yearning for Israel's future Messiah who would destroy our enemies and establish Israel as earth's dominant force.

Momentary bliss faded as my eyes lifted towards the single, most dominant blot on Bethlehem's landscape, Herod's fortress, the Herodian. My father had died, conscript labour in the gargantuan task of flattening that hilltop. Now, Herod's dark creation perched above Bethlehem, a giant, malevolent monster, staring silently; reminding always of Israel's slavish state.

Messiah will remedy that! I thought.

Laying the ram's horn on a large boulder, I stretched and realised I'd been too much dreaming. Not a good habit for a watchman. And with that thought I started my usual circuit around the hilltop where I could observe the sheepfold, the nearby road, a portion of our pastureland and the inn that marked boundary between pastureland and city.

The last of the itinerant Levites had passed through the inn's doors hours before. Levites arriving from all over Judea to assist the priests as they dealt with an influx of worshippers.

The last stragglers disappeared from the road below, which only a few hours previous had been filled with would-be worshippers seeking shelter.

Worshipers? The word brought sadness. While others worshipped in the temple, covered their sins with the blood of sacrifice, I had no means for covering my own.

Then, looking up at a shining moon surrounded by

shimmering stars, my melancholy evaporated in night's beauty. For certain I missed sharing in festivities of the moment, but duties involving oversight of Jehovah's flocks seemed Jehovah's will for me.

Under the illuminating sky I looked out on rolling hills surrounded in mysterious shadow, on the pattern of houses and streets in Bethlehem town, and on to the profiled walls and towers of Jerusalem. I breathed the pure air, inhaled the beauty and thought again, *So much better to be a shepherd here than tending sheep among profane ruffians in the wild lands of Judah.*

Below me, moonlight highlighted each paving stone laid by Roman engineers, and that sight returned me to not-so-beautiful thoughts. *Romans.* Bile rose in my throat. *When will Messiah come? How much longer can my people wait?*

Words of my namesake, the prophet Micah, intruded. Over one thousand generations before my time he'd declared that Bethlehem, insignificant Bethlehem, would be the birthplace of Messiah, *Ruler of Israel, Avenger of Wrongs.*

What if Messiah were born this night, on my watch?

15

Would I even know?

A shadow appeared on the moonlit roadway. The shadow grew as it left the streets of Bethlehem and continued on the Roman road paralleling our pasturelands and nearing the Inn of the Levites.

Foolish people travelling at night. They should know there would be no more chance of lodging beyond Bethlehem than within its confines. Those lurking in the shadows would as easily plunder a stranger as steal a sheep.

I straightened, wet my lips, and reached for the ram's horn as the moving shadow separated itself from the road and moved toward the sacred pasturelands. The moonlight now illuminated a man leading a donkey with a rider balanced on its back.

The urge to race down the hill and direct the man back to the road passed as the intruders paused at the inn. I knew the innkeeper, a brusque, no-nonsense type. *Good*, I thought. *He'll send them on their way.*

The man knocked on the door and the sound of his voice carried faintly to my ears. A muffled voice

16

answered. The door didn't open. *Good*!

But the man didn't turn towards the road. Instead his steps took him towards the lambing stable.

"Stop them Jehovah!" I prayed. "Stop them lest they defile the sacred space intended for your lambs alone."

I saw Eliezer, our lead shepherd, exit the stable, lamp held high, expecting the sound of his stern voice to order these trespassers on their way. Instead, the lamp moved nearer the intruders and the man leading the donkey dropped his lead rope, and eased its rider to the ground.

A lady! A lady, stumbling as her feet touched ground.

My heart nearly stopped when Eliezer took one arm, the man the other.

Eliezer touching a woman. No! No! It could not be.

Stunned, I watched Eliezer join the stranger in assisting the lady through the entrance of the lambing stable.

Forgetting my task of watchman, my panicked eyes

locked on the space meant only for sacred newborn lambs.

My mind rebelled at the thought of a woman in the same stable as our sacred lambs.

But my anger, disgust, and fear disappeared as stable, town and pasturelands dissolved in light. The sky bloomed, consuming and brilliant; birthing a moving form, a form defined in light of such piercing intensity one forgot the world of light in which it moved. A form floating over our pastureland.

Falling to my face, shaking hands covering both eyes, a voice of crystalline purity banished my fears.

"I bring good news, news meant for all peoples everywhere. A Saviour, Messiah, is born today, right here in Bethlehem, David's city. You will find the baby wrapped in strips of cloth and lying in a manger."

At the sound of those words I half uncovered my eyes to a vision of sky swirling with life, and music and voice. One voice? A thousand? But words I would never forget. "Glory to God above all and peace to His creation and to all those with whom He is pleased."

Then, light and voices receded, leaving pregnant silence behind. Peering out through parted fingers, eyes still half blind, I saw only moon, stars, and darkness. Bathed in euphoric memory, I lay still while savouring words of the celestial vision. A vision, quickly fading, as doubts crept in.

Could it really be? Had I, Micah, seen Messiah's mother and father! No! That could not be. Fragments of Torah, the Prophets and Midrash flashed through my mind. Messiah's mother would be a virgin. There could be no father.

Rolling onto my knees and looking downslope I saw shepherds standing frozen and still under the open stars above the sheep-fold. As still as Lot's wife who'd turned from being a frightened human to pillar of salt.

I bolted down the hill and joined a milling, clamouring group with being tossed about. All this confusion compounded by loud bleating from the sheepfold.

Then Thaddeus' voice over rode the din. "Quiet! We have heaven's instructions, *Go! See! Tell!*

Even those not seeing what I had, knew the way. I followed behind the others towards the birthing stable, my mind buffeted by scripture, rabbi's teaching, heaven's explicit words, and evidence of my own eyes.

Last through the stable opening I hesitated until bodies parted for a moment and I glimpsed a tall stranger standing beside the polished, white stone manger.

Forcing my way forward the whole scene came to life. A young woman, younger than me, lay on the stable floor with Eliezer's cloak around her.

I slipped between two other shepherds and stared down at a baby. A tiny hand and arm slipped from under swaddling cloth. A mouth opened, and I heard a cry, much like a bleating lamb.

On a Snowy Christmas Eve

by

Peter Coffey

On a snowy Christmas Eve,
With the kids tucked in bed,
The presents wrapped and hugs shared,
Our tree glittered and the star shimmered.

Eggnog and rum with a peppermint cane,
Elvis's "Here Comes Santa Claus" on the radio,
I turned down the lamp so the string lights glowed.
She nestled in beside me and took my hand.

With a twinkle in her eye,
My wife, my lover, my girl smiled that smile.
Warmness filled me on this cold winter night.
My heart pounded like reindeer hooves on a roof.

I took my Christmas gift in my arms.
Her sparkling eyes and candied lips met mine.
Off came her ugly holiday sweater,
Showing off her Yuletide beauty.

We clutched and grabbed and loved.
We fell to the floor by the crackling fire.
I was so into her and she down to me
We didn't hear the noise up the chimney.

The flames went out with a gust of air
As a large fat man landed on the embers,
His eyes went wide and his jaw dropped.
"Ho-ho-ho?" came from his bearded face.

We lay bare before Ol' Saint Nick.
Staring at each other, the fat man said,
"I see your ten year old Christmas wish came true."
"It sure did," I said with a grin.

He pulled out a sack of black filled with joy
And with a struggle, got out of the fireplace.
He stepped over us and headed to the evergreen.
"What is he talking about?" my love asked.

"It was ten years ago this holiday eve
I asked Santa to bring you back.
We'd had an awful breakup
And you came back that Christmas Day."

"Thank you, Santa Claus," we said together.
The big man in red dropped the last gift under the tree.
"My pleasure," he said and scooted up the fireplace.
"Merry Christmas to all," he shouted, grinning.

I looked at my lady – her face red as holly berries.
She beamed like a Nativity scene and said,
"It's a good thing the kids didn't see this Santa visit."
I nodded and heard, "Mom? Why are you naked?"

On that snowy Christmas Eve,
We laughed and shooed the boys back up to bed.
With a holiday we will never forget,
We wish you a happy Yuletide time!

A Big Boxco Christmas

by

Mike Dykstra

Leo, the Chief Henchman of Big Boxco (We Think Big So You Don't Have To) sighed. So many orphaned dollars floating around in the econosphere that needed a good loving home. Him who had the space and the will to provide a home.

His Vice President of Gratuitous Greed gently cleared his throat.

"Yes, George. What is it?"

"Erm, you summoned me your chief henchmanship."
The vice president knew that 'chief henchman' was an
oxymoron. However, he had seen too many rising
stars point this out. They were invariably rewarded for
their erudition with a promotion to Vice President of
the Big Boxco Dictionary project. The big Boxco
dictionary project was housed in a corner office which
turned out to be an elaborately disguised elevator
leading directly to a one-way exit.

The chief henchman also knew it wasn't really a thing.
However, he found it a useful tool to weed out the
tiresomely obsequious from those truly dedicated to the
art of keeping the boss happy.

"Yes. I wonder if you have any ideas on how to
maximize our Christmas sales?"

"I have many ideas, your honorific. Unfortunately,
most of them are nothing more than banditry in both
the literal and figurative sense."

"And this is a problem?"

"Ethically, no. Legally, yes. Neither you nor I would
thrive in a prison setting."

"It's too bad we can't have a second Christmases, complete with bereft orphans, a compelling back story and a natural villain," mused the Chief Henchman.

"A villain who isn't me," he added.

"Let me think about it, your villainous." the VPGG said.

Every week the VPGG called his brother, noted theoretical physicist Rafael Stoddard to see what was going on in the world of science. As the VPGG would point out to the very few people who asked him, this was in accordance with his mother's wishes—as they pertained to the distribution of her rather large estate.

The VPGG would often just let the phone sit on the couch while his brother spoke of sciency things that had very little opportunity for generating sizable amounts of money.

"What's new, Rafe?" he asked.

"I just got back from a physicist conference. Dr. Von Schlepping gave an inspired talk on the importance of inventing a workable way to travel through time."

"Why," the VPGG intoned, wondering if, perhaps, he had accorded his poor lamented mother's ability to monitor his telephone calls too much credence.

"Apparently Von Schlepping's great great great (etc) grandfather and/or grandmother was deprived of Christmas back in 1582 and this has caused a great deal of mental anguish to the family. He wants to right this great wrong."

"Deprived of Christmas," the VPGG gasped. "That's horrible. . all that money not spent on useless and unnecessary gifts. The horror. How did that happen?"

"Calendar reform," Rafael said.

"I should have known. Those Calendar guys are always messing with Christmas." The calendar manufacturing industry had, so far, refused Big Boxco's requests to shorten the number of days between Christmas and, in fact, every other excuse for gift giving. Big Boxco had considered making its own calendar but had yet to crack the secret of knowing which day fell on which date.

"Was Dr. Von Schlepping's ancestor by any chance an ummmm orphan."

"He didn't say."

"When did this happen?"

"1582."

"Suffice it to say then the parents are dead rendering the children, according to the Big Boxco dictionary, they are orphans. Gotta go. Talk to you next week, Rafe."

"But wait, we…."

The VPGG had hung up the phone, his mind churning with possibilities.

"So, your head henchmanship, we are seeking to address this great wrong by having the calendar rolled back to provide an extra Christmas on behalf of the poor children of 16th Century Belgium."

"With interest. It's been over 400 years, after all. Had we managed to cash in on that Christmas, we would be known as Gargantuan Boxco."

"With interest, then"

"How are you doing to pull this off?"

The VPGG smiled. He didn't want to share his secret weapon, the literally soulless lawyer, Alexander Clause. "Leave that to me. Sir."

Many have suggested that with a last name like 'Clause,' Alexander's future as a lawyer was preordained. This, of course, is utterly false as there are far more Clauses who aren't lawyers than are. Alexander's descent into the legal profession started in 2012 when he traded his soul for a 2006 PT Cruiser. The following day, he drove his new purchase to the university and enrolled in the faculty of law and discovered that he should have held out for a BMW or a Jag.

"If I Understand you correctly, Mr. Clause, you are advocating on behalf of some long-dead Belgic children who missed Christmas in 1582 due to Calendar reform and you feel that this is yet another past wrong that must be righted."

"Yes, your senatorship."

"And you are looking for someone in the house to act on behalf of these victims of vicious calendar reformers."

"Who may, or may not be," Alexander lowered his voice, quickly stealing a look at the party affiliation of Senator Smith, "democrats."

"And you are prepared to pay handsomely for this."

"We can pay you handsomely. We can pay you ugly as sin. We'll pay you however you want."

"All right, Mr. Clause, we have ourselves a deal."

There were times when Alexander regretted trading his soul for a 2005 PT Cruiser. However, at times like this, he was just glad that his soul wasn't present to see what he had become.

The same scene played out in offices on both sides of the great political divide.

And so it was that the greatest bipartisan compromise (excluding anything to do with their own compensation packages) passed nearly unanimously; the only exception being Senator Johnny Strep who had died during the voting process and inadvertently pressed the no button with his nose in doing so. A spokesman for the Senator insisted that the Senator's reasons for doing so were appropriate under the circumstances and he would be defending his actions in the upcoming election.

"Honey, what are we going to do about the Belgian Orphans."

Honey belched. "I don't know. Let the little bastards make their own way in life the same way my daddy and me did."

"They had Christmas stolen from them by the evil Calendar Reformers. We can't do nothing."

Honey grimaced. "I can't stand those calendar reformers. Did you see what they did to the calendar this year. Every page has a picture of an old man hugging his money. And the ones with nice pictures have the wrong days on them."

"Shall we go shopping, then. Buy some toys for the little urchins."

"It's the least we can do."

The Chief Henchman smiled. It was not a pretty sight. "George. The Belgian Christmas sales are even better than the real Christmas. We're selling calendars like never before—and even got some free publicity from the morality squad who find the March picture just a bit salacious—what can I say, I love money. What's happening with all of these gifts, anyway.

The VPGG shrugged. "Who cares. As long as we're selling them for a good markup."

The old man sat stunned. "You're like the son I never had."

The VPGG looked out the window where large snowflakes were softly falling over a Dickensian cityscape. "Thanks....your dadship."

It did raise an interesting question, though. What was being done with all the gifts being bought and donated to the Belgian Children's Christmas organization. His super greedy sense told him there was extra profit to be made off this. He'd have to ask his guy.

His guy, the venal and venerable Alexander Clause was driving around aimlessly in his fully restored 2006 PT Cruiser, hoping to trade it back for his soul, or any soul, really. He didn't really need the soul per se but felt that it was time to upgrade his ride and had his eye on a 1982 Plymouth K Car which was, spiritually, the ancestor to the PT Cruiser.

Alexander had confirmed with Dr. Von Schlepping that the likelihood of anyone inventing a practical method of actually delivering these gifts was insignificant. The good doctor's intention was admirably selfish in that he was trying to steer competitors away from his own field of research so he could win the Nobel prize.

The gifts were collected on behalf of the children, warehoused in buildings owned by Big Boxco, acquired from the bankrupt Calendar industry and rented out to the various charitable and government agencies tasked with bringing order to the Belgian Orphans plight at exorbitant rates.

They would be waiting for next year, if that actually had any meaning on the Big Boxco Calendar, when it would be announced that the children of Transylvania had also suffered an egregious theft of Christmas. In

1590, they skipped from December 14 directly to December 25th thereby depriving the merchants of last minute Christmas shoppers dropping piles of money for gifts to appease their starving children. All the Bobby and Betty the Belgian dolls would become Terry and Theresa the Transylvanian dolls and the accounting departments would sing with glee.

In an otherwise unremarkable laboratory in the middle of an otherwise unremarkable desert in the middle of an otherwise unremarkable continent, Dr. Rafael Stoddard ignored the ringing phone. Thursday at 5:00 meant it was probably his annoying brother. Rafael only accepted the calls because his mother's will had promised to fund his research if he was 'nice' to his ethically bereft brother.

Dr. Stoddard stared at the image on his Temporal Transmitter Device; at the happy Belgian family gleefully sharing gifts on the traditional gift day of January 7.

He thought, correctly, that his brother would not want to know about this.

All the more reason to go straight to the media.

Santa's Wild Ride

by

E.E. Judd

Santa looked at the collection of oddly shaped glass vases sitting on the chunky coffee table of an unkempt apartment. Light from the street glinted through the vases, casting a rainbow against the worn out sofa behind them. The whole room was littered with crumpled snack bags, gaming controllers, old socks and a box of half-eaten pizza and it stunk of a strange musky odor.

Perhaps he was just out of touch, but he really didn't understand the tastes of this generation. It was a hazard of being an immortal being, he supposed, sustained by nothing but hope and dreams. He felt old.

Ah well, Santa thought, turning away. *At least people still need me. For now.*

He set a neatly wrapped gift under a cheap fake tree, then straightened with a groan. His old sleigh injury was acting up again. It was going to be a long night.

He brightened. On a chair beside the tree, a glass of milk and plate of goodies sat on a handwritten note. *'Dear Santa,'* it read. *'Uncle Steve said that everyone loves his special brownies so I left some for you. Love, Adam.'*

What a kind child! He was supposed to be on a diet, but just one wouldn't hurt. Santa picked up a brownie and took a bite, sighing as the rich mint chocolate unfurled his tongue. Uncle Steve may be messy, but he was an excellent baker.

The second brownie quickly followed the first and he chased it all down with the glass of milk. Santa patted his belly with satisfaction. He hustled back to the magically created chimney and zipped up, popping out of the stack and landing on the roof. A quick check of his pocket watch showed eleven o'clock. Ahead of schedule! He climbed into his sled and grasped the reins.

"Away!" he cried. His reindeer pawed the roof and then in a great leap of muscle and magic, took off into the glittering sky.

House after house, gift after gift, Santa made his way across the globe. Time moved more slowly for immortal beings, and after another hour's work, he realized his journey was halfway done.

"We might finish early tonight," he called ahead to his reindeer.

They flicked their ears at him but kept their attention on navigating. Planes were a very real threat, and each reindeer had been trained in early identification as well as evasion techniques. For now, however, not a single plane or cloud marred the midnight sky.

"The stars are so beautiful," Santa whispered.

He stroked his beard and giggled at how soft it felt. He felt good. In fact, he felt amazing! He twisted experimentally. Even the pain from his injury had subsided. It was the magic of Christmas, he decided and melted into his seat.

***

The sound of hooves clattering on a rooftop jerked Santa awake. Had he fallen asleep? Milk and cookies! He knew he ought to be concerned about sleeping on the job, but a powerful sense of peaceful contentment sat on him like a heavy blanket and it was just too much work to care.

Santa languidly stretched and turned slightly to admire the sack of gifts towering in the back of his sleigh.

"Goodness, that's a big bag!"

It was magical, of course. No normal bag could hold all the gifts of the world. All he had to do was think of the receiver, reach his arm in, and magic would provide the correct parcel. A quick consult with his List told Santa he was at the house of Annette Butterfield, status: Nice. In fact, she was listed as having been Nice for fifty years in a row. Fifty whole years!

The sack handed over a box which his personal magic told him was a necklace set with gemstones.

"Now that's not right," he muttered, frowning.

Someone as wonderful as Annette deserves more than a

boring necklace. She must want something cooler. More modern. Something amazing for such a Nice girl!

He shoved the necklace back inside and willed for a gift that would make her happy. A different box came out this time, and when Santa focused on it he blushed. It certainly wasn't the usual toy he put under the tree, but... Well, why not? 'YOLO', as the kids would say.

"She'll be just delighted, eh boy?" he said to Donner, slapping the animal on the rump. Donner pinned back his ears and danced in place.

It occurred to Santa that he was acting strangely. But why? As per Mrs. Clause's stern reminder, he'd eating no treats that night except... The brownies. Perhaps Uncle Steve knew magic?

Resolving to investigate later, Santa eased back into his sleigh. He took up the reins and yelled, "On Dasher, on Dancer, on Comet and Blitzen! On... I don't remember all your names right now but on anyways!"

At the next house, Santa pulled a t-shirt out of his bag for ten-year-old Zach. Santa scratched his head under his cap, trying to work out what the writing on the front meant. No matter how he looked at it, he still didn't understand. Oh well, he knew that kids these days loved t-shirts. He put the gift upside-down beneath the tree then snuck back to the chimney, giggling at his prank.

He was still laughing to himself when he crawled out onto the roof. "I left it upside-down!" he chortled to the reindeer, wiping tears from his eyes.

Look at him being such a tricky trickster! He was hip. He was cool. He could keep up with the youth of today.

The sky grew lighter as Santa's journey neared its end, and he began to yawn continually. At each stop, it became harder and harder to pull himself out of his sleigh, as if his body was glued to its soft cushions. Finally, the last gift was delivered and he heaved a sigh of relief.

"Back we go," he said, feeling warm and happy at the thought of home.

Blitzen shook his head and pulled against his harness, clearly eager to return to his cozy barn and delicious oats. Santa sympathized. He was feeling mighty munchy himself.

"Hup boys, hup!" He gave a whoop as they took off.

His reindeer responded to a second gentle snap of

reins, sprinting in a wild dash across the stratosphere. Cold wind cut into Santa's face and made his eyes water, but he barely felt it, giddy with the feel of flying faster than he'd ever been. What else could they do?

"Loopty-loop!" he cried, pulling up.

The reindeer brayed in protest but obeyed, and within moments his sleigh climbed into the clouds. This high up it was so cold breathing hurt, and moisture hit his face in droplets that stung. Santa sputtered icy sleet from his mouth, wondering if perhaps this was a bad idea after all.

He was so preoccupied defending his face that he almost didn't notice Dasher and Dancer drop out of sight. He blinked stupidly for a moment or two, then realized that all his reindeer were dropping. The sleigh hovered for a moment and his heart floated up to his throat. Then he plummeted straight to the icy roads below.

"Milk and cookieeeeeeeeeeees!"

A massive gust of wind and bone-shaking roar tore the cap from his head. He looked up, holding onto his sleigh for dear life. The white underbelly of a plane flash by, its engines shredding the air right where he'd been barely a moment before. Then it disappeared into the night, leaving rumbles and spinning clouds in its wake.

The ground drew up fast. Suddenly the reindeer pulled up hard, sending the whole line into a whip that slammed Santa to the floor. The sleigh evened out and Santa shakily pulled himself back up, deciding to never, ever try sleigh tricks again.

They reached the North Pole before dawn. Santa climbed out of his sleigh with limbs that felt weighted with wet snow and drug himself into his cottage.

Mrs. Clause looked up as he entered. "Welcome back, dear. Was it a long night? Where's your hat?"

He could only stare at her stupidly. "I... I..."

Her familiar, kind eyes looked at him with concern. "Are you all right Mr. Clause? Would you like some hot chocolate to warm you up?"

He drew a slow breath. "I'd like to go to bed," he said.

"Really? Oh, thank heavens! You've had too many restless nights recently. I was starting to think I'd have to send one of the elves to a human pharmacy for sleep medication."

She hustled him off to bed, tucking him under the covers and kissing his bearded cheek. He sighed, feeling like he could sleep for months. He didn't know what had been in those brownies, but maybe Steve would be willing to share the recipe.

Santa smiled and closed his eyes.

***

Zach hopped down the stairs in his pajamas and raced over to the tree.

"Santa came!" he hollered up the stairs, then gleefully danced around the living room.

His mom and dad stumbled behind him, rubbing their faces and giving jaw-cracking yawns.

"Can I open my presents?" he asked.

His mom smiled and smoothed down his bedhead. "Just wait, Dad's getting the camera."

Zach pulled all his presents into a pile, counting and shaking them.

"Ok Zach, go ahead. Which one are you going to open first?"

"This one from Santa!"

He picked up a lumpy bundle and tore off the wrapping, bits of paper flying everywhere. He held it up in front of him. It was a t-shirt, black, with large numbers printed in white on the front. Zach wrinkled his nose in confusion.

"Dad, what does 4:20 mean?"

Christmas Concert

by

Pat Meek

A new school year is ahead of us. My schoolmates, in our grades one to eight country school, soon realize something special is planned for this year's Christmas concert. Our teacher, Mr. Smith, shares the script of the play, *Puss in Boots*. We have no notion of how far he will take this play or that he will take all of his students along for the ride.

The setting is the French court of Louis the XlV. We are assigned our roles. We memorize our lines. We rehearse our parts. *Puss in Boots* is a French fairy tale published in 1697 about a cat that uses trickery and deceit to gain power for his low born and impoverished master, Jack. Jack, the third son of a miller, receives the cat as his inheritance from his father. The elder brother gains the mill, the second brother, the mules. Such are the rules of inheritance at this time in history. The largest portion goes to the eldest and the allotment diminishes down the line until the youngest receives little.

The cat is no ordinary feline and is determined to gain a fortune for Jack. Splendid in boots and hat he makes gifts to the king on behalf of his master, the fictional Marquis of Carabas. With further deception and wild plots of Puss, the king becomes so impressed with Jack he awards him the princess in marriage. Thereafter, the cat enjoys life as a great lord who runs after mice only for his own amusement. It goes without saying; the Marquis and the princess live happily ever after.

My sister Jennifer is narrator of the play. Dressed in a long green gown she appears both masterful and vulnerable. At nine years of age she has already won public speaking awards. Classmate Don plays Puss. Mr. Smith fashions a cat's head for him from Paper Mache. Realistic. My older sister Shirley plays the princess and wears a pink, full-skirted gown, sewn by our mother. She looks out coyly from a hand held fan. I play the lowly miller, soon to benefit from the schemes of the clever Puss. My humble miller's clothes are later changed to those of the well-to-do, a coat and breeches of green with a lace jabot at my neck. I wear borrowed spectator pumps. For the court scenes we wear white, powdered wigs, fashioned by Mr. Smith. Our classmates, in their roles of king, queen, pages and guards comprise the rest of the cast.

In one court scene Shirley and I do the French Minuet. We sing as we dance:

> *When dames wore hoops and powdered hair*
> *And very strict was etiquette.*
> *When men were brave and ladies fair*
> *They danced the Minuet.*
>
> *Slippers high heeled with pointed toe*
> *Trod stately measures to and fro.*
> *With head held high and bowing low*
> *They danced the Minuet.*

John Williams, the Nipawin High School drama teacher, hears what we are doing and pays a visit to a dress rehearsal. He, in turn, contacts Mary Ellen Burgess, Drama Consultant at the University of Saskatchewan. She visits to see the play for herself. Mrs. Burgess extends an invitation. We are invited to present at the Saskatchewan High School Drama Festival in Saskatoon. We won't be in competition for we are not a high school, but we will be the opener for the rest of the program.

We travel to Saskatoon in March. (Many of us have never travelled so far from home). It's a lovely spring day with snow melting in the warm sun. We eat at the Commodore Restaurant, perform the play and make our way home the next day. This is a very special experience thanks to a creative teacher, his wife, and the many parents who help. We are blessed.

My only purchase in Saskatoon is a yellow 45 rpm recording of *Thumbelina.*

I play it on our gramophone as soon as I get home.

> *Thumbelina, Thumbelina, tiny little thing*
> *Thumbelina dance, Thumbelina sing.*
> *What's the difference if you're very small?*
> *When your heart is full of love*
> *You're nine feet tall.*

Mom comes downstairs and tells me I am keeping everyone awake. I am told to go to bed. Even budding stage stars must take direction from their mothers.

A Christmas To Remember

by

Joan Mettauer

The turkey was cooked to perfection–the skin dark brown and crispy, the white meat juicy and tender. Its mouth-watering, poignant aroma seeped under the doorway of the tiny, sixth floor apartment and down the narrow, dimly lighted hallway. It flowed across worn, thread-bare carpeting and into the sad, cheaply furnished neighbouring suites, causing more than one lonely resident to close his or her eyes and long for the days when Christmas was merrier . . . when there had been something to celebrate, and someone to celebrate with.

On December 23, Emily (the sole occupant of apartment number 603) had impulsively decided to orchestrate her first holiday dinner. She declared that *she,* being the hostess, would supply the turkey, and each of her guests would bring something to contribute to the Christmas Day meal.

Julia was Emily's best friend and co-worker. She was, if Emily cared to admit it (which she never would), the *only* friend she'd made since moving to The Big Smoke a year ago. Most newcomers to Toronto had no idea what the nickname of Canada's largest city meant, and were either too embarrassed to ask or didn't really give a damn. Julia fit into the latter category. Her contribution to the festive holiday dinner was mashed potatoes. She arrived at Emily's early in the afternoon bearing ten pounds of Russet spuds. She proceeded to peel, cook and mash them while the two women gossiped about everyone else in their office. Emily grimaced when Julia added an overly generous half pound of butter and a pint of whipping cream to the cooked potatoes and beat the concoction until it was smooth and creamy. Mashed potatoes were one of Emily's biggest diet downfalls, but she suspected that Julia wanted to make them extra-delicious just for her. After all, that's what best friends do.

Emily had befriended Taylor quite by accident soon after moving to Toronto to begin her new job. Determined to develop a svelte physique and shed twenty pounds, Emily joined the neighbourhood gym the same day she'd signed the lease on her apartment. Taylor, her long blond hair in direct contrast to Emily's severely spiked raven locks, was six inches taller and forty pounds lighter than Emily. She ran loose-limbed and effortlessly on the treadmill adjacent to Emily's and hadn't given the newcomer a second glance–until Emily tripped and flew off the walking belt, landing in an ungracious heap on the floor. Somehow an unlikely alliance had developed between the two opposites. Sarah had met them for drinks a couple times and seemed to really like her too, which pleased Emily. Taylor, who didn't cook, had volunteered to bring pumpkin pie, dinner buns and cranberry sauce. The whole-wheat buns and pie were from Wal-Mart, the cranberry sauce in a can.

Joshua and Sarah lived together on the second floor of Emily's apartment building and were the only other residents that Emily met socially since she'd moved in. Chatting at the lobby mailboxes had developed into dropping by each other's apartments for an occasional coffee, which segued into a glass of wine and eventually a friendship of sorts. Joshua, fit and tanned, worked at a sports and outfitters store while Sarah, who was an American but held a Canada Green Card, was a barista at a popular coffee haunt a few blocks away. She and Josh had met while he was on a holiday in the U.S. two years ago and they had been together ever since. Sarah loved to cook, and if truth be known so did Joshua. They both jumped at the invitation to Christmas dinner and arrived at the door bearing a steaming sweet potato casserole swimming in butter and brown sugar and dotted with pecan halves, and a covered dish of creamed peas and carrots.

Matthew's invitation had been unplanned and issued at the last minute. Emily had dropped down to the corner liquor store on Christmas Eve afternoon to pick up a bottle of wine. She didn't drink the stuff herself, preferring a good old vodka and OJ, but thought she should have a bottle on hand in case one of her guests neglected to bring their own. Matthew worked at the liquor store and Emily had spoken to him dozens of times over the past year. He seemed nice, always courteous and helpful. He was easy on the eyes, too. While he was ringing up Emily's purchase she'd jokingly said, "So, if you're not doing anything for Christmas dinner tomorrow you're welcome to join us. I'm having a few friends over." For a moment he appeared taken aback, but in the next breath he asked for her address and what time he should arrive. Matthew brought a bag of salad greens, a bottle of Ranch dressing, a big 1.5 litre bottle of white wine, and a small bottle of Niagara Icewine he claimed was to die for. He declared he would it himself, with dessert.

The guests, most of them strangers to each other, all arrived earlier than planned. Perhaps they were anxious to cement their individual, tenuis relationship with their hostess, or maybe they wanted time for their nerves to calm before dinner. Whatever the reason, Emily was surprised to find her small apartment crowded with near-strangers a good hour before the bird was ready to make its grant exit from oven to platter.

While they waited, introductions were made, drinks poured and a bowl of buttery homemade nuts 'n bolts (Emily's grandmother's recipe) devoured. Stiff shoulders relaxed and strained conversations began to first trickle, then flow with unbounded ease. By the time the turkey was cooked, its stuffing exhumed, and the gravy strained and thickened, the small apartment was filled with easy and generous laughter that bordered on becoming boisterous.

The new friends crammed together around Emily's square kitchen table, which she'd adorned with a festive red tablecloth and two tall, red tapered candles. They each took a seat before one of the five carefully arranged place settings, none of which matched. In spite of this, the table looked lovely and was overflowing with the sliced turkey, mashed potatoes, stuffing, sweet potato casserole, creamed peas and carrots, tossed salad, dinner buns and cranberry sauce. Bowls were passed around and dinner plates filled to overflowing. Wine glasses and drinks were topped up. Her five guests agreed that Emily's turkey stuffing was the best they'd ever eaten–moist and perfectly seasoned–but when asked to share her recipe she only smiled benignly. But she glowed. Yes, she was pleased with the unexpected compliment. With her *success*. She gazed around the small table with slightly blurry eyes, wondering if her guests were as completely contented as she was.

~JULIA~

How the hell did she manage to find four other suckers to invite for dinner? I thought I was the only one who could put up with Emily's whining. All she ever does is complain about how expensive Toronto is and how she hates the noise and the traffic. Why doesn't she just go back to that godforsaken Saskatchewan she claims to miss so much? If she wasn't my supervisor and such a gossip I'd tell her to stuff her stupid turkey dinner where the sun don't shine. Stupid bitch. Inviting me to stupid Christmas dinner after I told her a thousand times that I HATE Christmas. I hope she gains ten pounds tonight. I wonder what time I can get out of here.

~TAYLOR~

Where in the world did Em find Matthew? He's the most gorgeous hunk of manhood I've seen in a long time. It doesn't look like they're an item–he hasn't paid a lot of attention to her. I wonder if she would be upset if I tried to take him home. I haven't had a really fun night in ages. Should I ask her first or just go for it? Oh Julia, don't offer Emily another helping of potatoes and gravy! It'll take the poor girl a week to work off the extra calories from this dinner.

~JOSHUA~

God damn! I had no idea boring old Emily had such a hot friend! Wonder why she hasn't brought that luscious blond babe around before? Looks like I'm gonna have to take out a membership at that gym Taylor is raving about. Maybe I'll be able to get a little more action than I do at home. Sarah's always taking extra shifts at work . . . I might as well put my spare time to good use. Good thing this ugly table cloth covers my crotch. I won't be able to get up til my buddy here settles down again!

~SARAH~

*Josh has been staring at Taylor all night. I wonder if he suspects. What if he **knows?** He can't though . . . I haven't said a word to anyone. Good God, I can hardly admit it to myself. I didn't plan for this to happen–it just did. Oh Taylor, I love you so much I think I'm going to die. What am I going to do? I wonder if you feel the same way about me. I think I'll tell Josh tonight. There's no use pretending any longer.*

~EMILY~

This is just the very best day of my life! Finally, I've made some good friends. I was starting to think it would never happen. Look at them! I love these guys!

Taylor seems to be getting along so well with Sarah and Josh. And Julia looks so happy; I'm so lucky she's my bestie! I wonder if she knows that Matthew has been sneaking a few peeks at her. He has such gorgeous brown eyes. I can't wait til Monday gets here! Julia and I are going to have so much to talk about during lunch. Maybe I'm going to like Toronto after all. We should all get together for New Year's Eve . . .

~MATTHEW~

What an annoying bunch of losers. Thank God the food is good. It's been a long time since anyone cooked a turkey dinner for me. I haven't had one since . . . since Mom kicked me out and told me she never wanted to see me again. Stupid bitch. That waste-of-air Julia reminds me of my dear old mama. I think I'll pick Julia tonight. Yeah . . . Julia. I think she'll do quite nicely. I see how she stares at me when she thinks I'm not looking. And she's so damn annoying. Em is a sweet innocent. I can tell Julia hates her. I can tell by the look in her evil eyes. Julia, I'll make you a very special glass of icewine tonight. Slip in a hit of Special K. Follow you home. Merry Christmas, Julia. Say good-bye to your new friends.

Christmas in Emergency

by

Murray Peters

I dread this day, this Christmas day. Suicides, car accidents, heart attacks – it doesn't stop for any day. And on this day, it's worse. Who wants to remember every year on December 25th that their loved one died? Not me. Yet I remember all those E.R. deaths every year. And here I was in Emergency on Christmas once again.

My first case was a 16 month old crying and tugging at her ears. A quick examination determined she had an ear infection. An anti-biotic cleared it up.

Second, a heart attack turned out to be indigestion quickly remedied by Pepto-Bismol.

Next, an elderly lady slipped on some ice and struck her head on the concrete outside her house. Her scalp had split open, and seven stitches closed the wound. I examined her for concussion symptoms: None. Still I ordered her to get some rest, but she insisted she had to attend Christmas dinner. And she was off.

Suicide attempts are a real problem at Christmas time. Here it was no different. A lonely young man saw no reason to go on living. He believed no one cared for him. He had taken a bottle of sleep aids and drank a mickey of vodka. A deadly combination. He was going to be my first death on this Christmas day.

We induced vomiting and injected him with an I.V. solution with the sleep aid anti-dote. His breathing slowed, and he lost consciousness. He was going down. His heartbeat slowed. Damn this season.

His mother was contacted, and she said she'd leave for the hospital immediately. Someone did care for him. Would we have to tell her her son died on Christmas day?

She arrived a half an hour later, and I took her aside. "Mrs. Adams, Lucas took a large dose of sleeping pills and alcohol. It was tense, but he'll survive. Thankfully."

"Thank you, doctor. Thank you." She hugged me.

It was 8pm. I was done my shift. No deaths this year on Christmas day. It's been a good day. Merry Christmas, everybody!

What's in a Name?

by

Martin Povey

There were just the three of them in his private chamber.

The others were waiting next door in the Great Ice Hall.

"So, it's like this" Rudolph said, shuffling his hooves as he focused intensely on the tinsel star just above Santa's head.

"It's like what" replied Santa, tapping his fingers on the arms of his throne, "C'mon man, spit it out".

"Yes, well, that's the point".

"What is the point?", fingers drumming faster.

"The man part".

Santa just sighed.

"I umm, I...well, I'd like to be called Rhonda".

"Rhonda" said Santa flatly, fingers suddenly still.

"Umm, yes, Rhonda."

Rudolph silently, slowly counted the points on the tinsel star.

"one... two... three... four... five"

Silence.

Rudolph counted again.

"one… two… three… four… five"

Still no response.

"one… two… three"…………..

The silence was suddenly shattered by Donner snickering.

"Rhonda?" repeated Santa.

Rudolph took a deep breath, tore his gaze away from the tinsel star and looked Santa straight in the eyes.

"Yes. Rhonda!" he said.

"And you?" said Santa warily to Donner, really not wanting to deal with this, "I guess you want to be called Delores or something."

"Oh no. No…no…no. Not me. I'm good. I'm Donner through and through. Yep, that's me Donner. Donner, I'm that. Yep, all the way. That's me. No Delores for me. I'm just…."

"Yeah yeah, OK." interrupted Santa.

"…here to support him, umm her, er, they."

He turned back to Rudolph. "So tell me son…

"No, not son, daughter maybe but I'm not quite….

"Whatever?...how did?... where did?…I mean what's going on here?"

"Well, I've never really felt, like,100% right being a guy reindeer ever since I knew anything about being a guy reindeer" blurted out Rudolph "Then about a year ago I decided to change my diet. I started grazing on special herbs and leaves, working out differently, my antlers began to shrink a bit. …it all just seemed the right thing to do. Things began to change. It was how I saw things. My attitude toward others and situations. I felt different. The way I think I was meant to be."

His voice shaking, Rudolph took another deep breath, "And then…and then something awful, wonderful…I mean scary and incredible happened. And I just couldn't hide the new me anymore. What am I saying?... I didn't want to hide the new me anymore!"

Santa leaned forward, his hand gently stroking Rudolph's ear, reassuring him, calming him down. "Tell me what happened" he spoke gently.

"My nose…my nose…it was turning pink."

There was a snicker again from Donner which was promptly cut short by a withering look from Santa.

"Carry on" said Santa.

"I thought that would be the end. I mean to all the kids in the world, to you, to all the other reindeer, to everyone, I'm supposed to be Rudolph the Red Nosed Reindeer. Not the one with the pink nose! But I want to be, have to be, Rhonda the Pink Nose Reindeer. I feel really good about myself for the first time in my life. You know, the way I was supposed to be. The real me."

Rudolph waited.

Donner waited.

"You've talked about this with the others, have you?"

"They all know" said Rudolph, "Most of them are supportive of me wanting to be the real me."

"So where do we go from here?" asked Santa. "What do you want from me?"

"To be honest, I hadn't really thought that through too much, my big thing was to get it off my chest. To hope that you would understand. Even to accept me as pink nosed reindeer. I couldn't even focus on preparing the routes for this year's deliveries."

Santa nodded. "Well, I've got to tell you it's a bit of a shock although, I must say that I had noticed your nose seemed much paler. I respect your decision of course and as you know, we acknowledge and respect diversity here at the North Pole. Heck, we've got several thousand vertically challenged workers!"

Rudolph chuckled, thinking of all Santa's elves.

"Every year on my travels around the world I see great changes in our societies. And along with those changes, more openness, greater understanding, acceptance and tolerance."

"I think the world could be ready to accept a pink nosed reindeer. Anyway, I'm just philosophizing now, so enough of that", said Santa, "Let's go and join the others, I'm sure they're all waiting to find out what happened in here."

Rudolph, Santa and Donner walked through into the Great Ice Hall where the rest of Santa's reindeers were gathered. Muted conversations stopped as the three of them entered.

"Rudolph and I have spoken" announced Santa, "And from this moment forward he, or rather, they, will be known as Rhonda - Rhonda the Pink Nosed Reindeer. What say all of you? All in favour say aye."

There was an excited chorus of cheers. Rhonda's pink nose perked up with pride. "Aye" they shouted one after another, "Aye" they cried. All of Santa's reindeer, that was, except one.

"I can't"…I just can't" spoke Vixen shaking his head.

The Great Ice Hall fell silent. Seven sets of antlers swung towards Vixen.

"Oh crap" thought Santa, "Here we go, I should have known." Only Mrs. Claus knew that Vixen was Santa's least favourite reindeer.

"It's abhorrent. It's not right." said Vixen, "We were made in His image. This is wrong! Firstly, it's not natural, secondly the world knows Rudolph as Rudolph with a red nose, not pink, and thirdly…and thirdly, well, it's just not right."

Nobody spoke. Rhonda walked slowly over to Vixen and gently nuzzled him with her antlers.

"There is no wrong Vixen. There is no right. We can all be the same. We can all be different. We don't need to be categorized, do we? Can't we just be? We are who we are. What we are. What we choose to be.

What we are chosen to be. I feel blessed because I have been chosen to be what I am. And I have chosen to accept this. Equally, you are blessed to be who and what you are. I'm still me Vixen, just a different version of me. And my new version loves you as much as the old version, don't you see?"

"I wanna be known as Danielle" shouted Dasher breaking the tension in the Hall.

"Put me down for Justin" said Dancer.

"Justin?" laughed Comet.

"Oh, OK then, how about Deborah."

"And I'll take Priscilla" Prancer jumped in.

"I like the sound of Claire" cried Comet.

"And I just love the sound of Caroline" said Cupid.

"And I'll be Donna" Donner threw in.

"But you're already Donna" said Dasher

They all laughed except Vixen

"No, not Donner like Donner, I mean Donna! Donna with an A."

"Put me down for Brittany" said Blitzen.

"Hey Vixen" called out Prancer, "What about you, what do you want to be called."

The Great Ice Hall fell silent.

Vixen scowled but said "OK, I'll play your game if I have to. I guess I could be Veronica."

As the team started singing Rhonda the Pink Nosed Reindeer, Rhonda turned back to Vixen smiling, "Vixen" she said, "I really want to thank you for..."

"Shut up you perverted, pink nosed piece of pig shit" hissed Vixen. "Just make sure you stay at the front of the rig. Stay way away from me you hear? I don't want to be riding anywhere near some transgender weirdo, you got it?"

Reeling back, Rhonda's eyes opened wide.

She dipped her head as she turned away.

A solitary tear trickled down towards her nose.

As it touched...that glowing pink beacon of pride and hope, faded to black.

Christmas's True Meaning

by

Katherine Smithson

Snow flakes falling with icy roads appearing,
indicates the season which many dread.
Yet when the stores get out their decorations
And Christmas Carols are heard
It becomes the most magical time of year.

With the trees all a glow,
Snowflakes glistening in the moonlight
Covering the land
In a white blanket of sparkles.

I am reminded of years long past

With a snowball fight breaking out,
Freeing the inner child in the elderly,
Followed by the exhilarating ride down,
A hill onto the frozen pond.

Where skating was met as a fun pass time
For all ages along the river trail.

As that special time of year draws near,
Stresses become the norm
As everyone rushes to and fro
In hopes of obtaining that best material gift.
Delivery's pick up
To help speed up
The arrival of something more.

Stores are stocked up
To meet the coming rush,
Making one wonder
What really matters?

And yet its when you sit around the tree

After the gifts are opened,
That the true meaning shines through.

We get so caught up in the hustle and bustle
Getting all of the years top items
Only to become old and outdated
By the time Christmas comes again.

That's when we loose sight
of the truth
Of spending time with those
Who are dear.

As kids we lay awake for a month
In anxious waiting
For what the Man in the red suit,
Will bring us next.
Its been said that children will remember times of love,
Where as the gifts received are the failing grades.

So why not put aside our greed
And focus on what really matters to us all?
Why not bring back the true meaning of Christmas
By sharing with those we treasure most?

Christmas Magic

by

Katherine Smithson

Sleigh bells ring,
As the horse trudges along
the freshly fallen snow.

A winter wonderland appears
Where the sparkling white forest
Covers the emerald green awaiting the sun.

Hibernation appears for those who refuse to see
The beauty of winter.
A hidden landscape appears covered,

In a layer of white diamonds.

Frozen ponds beckon now
to the inner child of us all,
Saying " Come out and play one and all"

Jack Frost makes his debut
With the icicles hanging amongst the branches
Creating beauty out of something so cold.

All this, is in preparation for Christmas.
a time for joy and fun.
For the kid in us all.
As the day comes near
When Santa comes with presents galore
For each good child.

Yet each year the list of wants is all too long.
Frantic shoppers rush the stores
Snatching up all the latest
Only to have the items forgotten
Come the following year.

Yet the snows still comes
beckoning us all to come out and play.

Instead we each lock the door
Closing the blinds
To the layer of white that now becomes our world,
Each longing for the warmth of the summer sun.

Yet amongst the chill of Winter,
Christmas has its own warmth
In the blazing fire on cool night.
With loved ones gathered near
We do recall memories of times long past.

Its when we shut out the snow
that we forget
The diamond layer of freshly fallen snow
Accompanied by the jingle of sleigh bells
Asking us all the question
Of how many get the chance to see sparkling snow
In the moonlight?
How many get to relive the snowballs
With loved ones?

Christmas is the time of year
We make memories to share
Around the meal we all help to prepare
With loved ones gathered near.

Christmas treats of long past,
Fill our senses again
With the watering of mouths
In the anxious anticipation
That always sends our taste buds to heaven and back.

The sights and sounds take us all back
To the true meaning of Christmas
Along with the magic
That does exist for children of all ages.

Our inner child rejoices
Each time its allowed out
To relive those long lost memories,
With the creation of new ones
That accompany the old.

Changes occur throughout the year
And its at Christmas time
We reflect on what has shaped
Our lives that matter
When the snow flakes fall
And the bells begin to jingle
In the release of Christmas Magic.

A Christmas Angel

by

Katherine Smithson

Snow flakes glistening,
Carols are sung around a warm fire in the hearth
Keeping out the chill of winter.

A tree of lights all aglow,
With presents for all underneath.
Yet as I gazed down at all the names
One was missing that Christmas Eve.

Where was mine?

I wondered as I searched and searched.
Only to find nothing, nothing at all.
Yet surely I did deserve one?
I had never been off the list ever before.

And so with a heavy heart
Of being forgotten about,
I hung my stocking with out a care
Neglected at Christmas was no fun.

Off into a troubled sleep,
Of having been forgotten about
Only to awaken to the warmth of the sun
All too soon.

At the curtains refused to keep out the sun
Awaking me with growl.
Was that low growl me or something else?
Quickly I threw back the covers,
Dashing out the door,
Nearly tripping over a small creature
Who came to attack the belt of my robe
Still undone.

A cat all orange and black

Was soon seen rubbing herself against my leg,
Marking her territory.

Smiling I picked her up wiping away a tear
As she curled up
And her loud diesel motor began.

Cheers and laughter came from all of us,
And I looked at the red bell collar
Where the name "Angel" sparkled in the morning light.

 A Christmas Angel she was at that.
She never left my side from that day on
Claiming me as her human.

She was the one who got the gift
Which I happened to be.

She was mine now
Where none were allowed to get near me
That day at all.
With her post moved from the beside the tree,
She did not leave.
Before long I was covered,
In the orange and black fur,

Of a tortoiseshell cat.

My nephew's two favourite colours.
Marked the gift curled on my lap.

I knew now
That I had never been forgotten at all
As the days went by
I would wake each morning
In praise of the angel
That slept beside me.

In times of a bad dream,
She was right there with a paw to the face,
Aware of my distress.

Every time Christmas comes again,
I looked at the cat all curled up
On my lap as I watch another rerun
Of one of the Santa Clause movies.
Family beside us all,
She was the reminder of when I had been forgotten about
Only to discover that it was her who had been forgotten instead.

A stray rescued she was the best gift ever to be received.

Angel was an accurate name for her.
With only a small speck of white on the tip of her tail,
She was an angel in fur.
Showing me that the best gifts
Don't need to come from a box under the tree
But from the love of a family,
With a desire to fix a rough year
With an addition of a furry companion.

Remembering the Christmas Magic

by

Katherine Smithson

Trees sparkle amongst the twinkling lights
As the land lay now in a sparkling blanket of white.

Not much of a sight if you look wrong.
Many will only feel the chill that comes
Whenever the strong north wind blows
But for the trained eye
Its magic that greets us instead.

Frost forms on the windowsills,

With the trees glistening in the glow.

Jingling of sleigh bells excites
The kid in us all.
Young or old
The bells remind of us all
Of the jolly fat man in the red suite
Pulled by either eight or nine reindeer.
Depending upon the weather
Christmas Eve brings

Santa Clause pulls to a stop,
At every house the world over
Delivering presents from sack.

After spending all year making them all
And checking the list twice
To ensure the magic of a Christmas comes
To all in one night with the sleigh piled high
And soaring over the globe
Where reports of the sightings are heard
Followed by the parents desperate plea
For children to sleep so that the magic can work.

As we grow older the story

Of Rudolph guiding the sleigh,
Seems to be for only the young.

Yet the message remains clear,
If we can show the world we aren't afraid
To believe in ourselves and others
We can too find a glowing light
Amongst the darkness.

All it takes is looking beyond
What our adult vision shows us
Allowing our inner child to take over
To remind us of the magic of Christmas
As freshly fallen snow glistens in the moon light,
With the chill in the air
The magical jingle of sleigh bells
Releasing the joy of Christmas.

Christmas Memories

by

Lillian Torrie

As I sit all alone in my comfortable home
I'm dreaming of Christmases past,
And the memories so dear of Christmas each year
· Are the ones that I want to hold fast

When I'd wake Christmas morning sometimes it was
storming;
But sometimes I'd look up above
When the sun, not quite risen, like light through a
prism

91

Gave suggestion of peace and of love.

Then off we would go, through sunshine or snow,
To the church on that most holy day.
After pre-Christmas riot we'd sit and be quiet:
"Peace on earth to all people," we'd pray.

A quick breakfast , and then we would gather again
'Round the tree we had trimmed with such care;
And our spirits would lift while exchanging each gift.
The excitement seemed too much to bear.

There was sometimes a game; of course never the same
As any we'd had from before.
I knew that with friends, I'd spend hours on end,
And still wish for "only one more."

There were usually new clothes (I could always use
those),
And for sure there'd be. books that were new.
Whether happy or sad, what adventures they had:
"Maida's Little---"; "Anne of---"; "Nancy Drew".

The rest of the day was spent mostly in play.
It was so for the children at least.
Of course, for my Mom, her duties weren't done:

She had to prepare for the feast.

Sometime after five would the neighbors arrive;
Mother, Father, and good-looking boy.
(Oh, yes, even back there I was fully aware
Of that guy, though I tried to act coy).

For adults, drinks and smokes, while the kids had their
cokes,
'Til at last came the call, "Dinner's ready!"
Food was set on the table and each person was able
To approach, sometimes just not quite steady.

Of these times I relate, the war years were not great
As we thought of the lads 'cross the sea;
When so many boys were denied Christmas joys
So their families at home would be free.

But most of my memories of joyful assemblies
And wonderful Christmases past,
And the wishes of cheer for another great year
Are my thoughts I'm so thankful that last.

cc. December 2014

Thank You

Thank you for buying and reading this book and for trusting us to entertain you. We hope you'll consider writing a blurb about *Jingle: A Christmas Anthology* on Amazon in the book listing's review section. It would be a huge honor if you did! And very much appreciated!

Best Christmas wishes always,
The Medicine Hat Rhyme & Reason Writers' Club

12509698R00053

Made in the USA
Middletown, DE
23 November 2018